WHAT HAPPENS NEXT?

Talent Show Troubles

JESS SMART SMILEY

:01 First Second
NEW YORK

CAST OF CHARACTERS

MEGAN

MEMBER OF SUNBRIGHT MIDDLE SCHOOL'S STUDENT GOVERNMENT

MR. FISHER

VICE PRINCIPAL AT SUNBRIGHT MIDDLE SCHOOL

GREG

VINCENT

SEAGULLS

ALWAYS OUT TO GET MEGAN

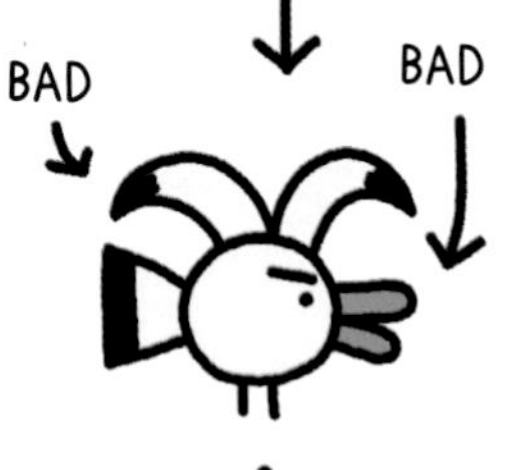

OLIVIA

TODD

- HOW TO - READ THIS BOOK

STEP 3 GO TO YOUR CHOSEN PAGE TO FIND OUT WHAT HAPPENS NEXT!

NO. WAY.

GOT IT? LET'S TRY IT OUT!

HMM...

YOUR CHOICES

STILL CONFUSED? READ THIS PAGE AGAIN.	READY TO START? GO TO PAGE 1.

NO!
SKWONK
LEAVE ME ALONE!!
JUST GO AWAY!
RUN AWAY
GO TO PAGE 9
HIDE
GO TO PAGE 17

ASK DAD TO ANNOUNCE
GO TO PAGE 102

DO IT YOURSELF
GO TO PAGE 82

TELL OLIVIA TO ANNOUNCE
GO TO PAGE 69

HELP OLIVIA WITH THE ANIMALS
GO TO PAGE 86

GO BACK TO ANNOUNCING
GO TO PAGE 137

IS THERE AN ELEPHANT?
NO.

IS THERE AN ESCALATOR?
NO.
A DUMBWAITER?
NO.
WHAT'S THAT?

TRAPDOOR?
NO.
A PORTAL?
NO.
DO I HAVE POWERS?
NO—YOU'RE JUST YOU.

CAN I TIME-TRAVEL?
NO.
DO I HAVE A PHONE?
NO.
IS ANYONE ELSE IN THE ROOM?
NO.
AM I A GIANT?
NO.

CAN I TRY?
?
GO TO PAGE 195

HONK!!!

I TOLD YOU—I'M HURRYING!
YEESH.

NK! HONK!
NOM
NOM NOM

HONK
I'M COMING! I'M COMING!

HONK HONK HONK

GO TO PAGE 48

YAY!
TWIRL
WOW!

THANK YOU FOR AN **AMAZING** TALENT SHOW!

AND SO...
HONEY—WE'RE SO **PROUD** OF YOU!
YOU KNOW, MOM—

—TODAY WAS A PRETTY GOOD DAY!
THE END

RUN TO BUS

GO TO PAGE 226

KEEP WALKING

GO TO PAGE 87

GIRLS
RESTROOM
OKAY.
JUST—
—JUST GIVE ME ONE SECOND...

WHOOPS!

YES! I MADE IT OUT!
SNOW HUT
WAIT A MINUTE— IS THAT DAD?
CLIMB BACK IN WINDOW
GO TO PAGE 23
HIDE
GO TO PAGE 37

MEGAN.
HUH?
GO TO PAGE 42

UGHHHH...
ZOMBIE!!
OH NO.

OLIVIA!
GRUH
BRUH
BLUG

BROOF!
?
MEGAN? NOOO!

MY BABY'S BEING CHASED BY A ZOMBIE!
GO TO PAGE 25

NUDGE
NUDGE
HRF
HM
HUP
GO UPSTAIRS
GO TO PAGE 144
GO TO KITCHEN
GO TO PAGE 219

CREEEEAK
PAGE 101
USA
FR. ROOM
KITCHEN
6 MOS
DAD CAVE
AW, MAN.
MEGAN'S FAMILY'S GARAGE

CHARLOTTE NEVER BROUGHT IT BACK!
HMPH!
YEAH, SHE'S MY BEST FRIEND—BUT SHE'S STILL FORGETFUL!
NOW WHAT AM I SUPPOSED TO DO?
WALK TO SCHOOL
GO TO PAGE 60
STAY HOME
GO TO PAGE 28

SPUK
SPLK
UGH!
WHAT'S THAT SMELL?
BLURP
SPUK
SPUK
SO GROSS...
yes—
A LIGHT!
WHOOPS!
TRIP
SPLUCK
MUST...
...Keep...
...GOING...
HUFF
HUFF
HUFF
yes...
...FINALLY...
GO TO PAGE 44

THANKS!

AND THEN I JUST—
WHOOPS!

DON'T BE ALARMED...
THIS IS ALL...
...PART OF THE TRICK...

HA
HA
HA
HA
HA
HRNGH!
HURR!
THIS IS AMAZING!
I KNOW!

GO TO PAGE 15

HOLD ON...
CHEW CHEW CHEW
HA HA HA HA HA HA HA
HA-HAH!
THAT WAS NOTHING...
CHECK THIS OUT!
WHAT THE...
IS HE DOING A HANDSTAND AND WHISTLING?!
I'M CONFUSED—SINCE WHEN CAN MR. FISHER DO COOL STUFF?
TAKE OVER GO TO PAGE 153
SIT AND WATCH GO TO PAGE 189

HUFF
HUFF
HUFF
WHAT? WHY DID YOU STOP?
!
WE CAN'T JUST LEAVE VIOLET!
SNATCH!
THEN I'LL DRIVE.
NICE TRY.
SUNBRIGHT HIGH SCHOOL
HURRY UP!!
COME ON!
THINK WE'LL MAKE IT IN TIME?
GO TO PAGE 91

HUFF
HUFF
HUFF
HUFF
PERFECT...
I CAN HIDE HERE!
SHF!
?
GO TO
PAGE 20

POUND
POUND
MEGAN?
IS THAT YOU?
?

THIS WASN'T PART OF THE PLAN...
OKAY.
ACT NATURAL.
GULP!
GO TO PAGE 68

GO TO PAGE 135

PHEW!
THAT WAS CLOSE—
SKRAWK
SKRAWW
HUFF HUFF
NO!
PLEASE!
LEAVE ME ALONE!
THE END

SNIFF
SNIFF
-NIBBLE-
CLICK
CLICK
CLICK
GO TO PAGE 181

GO GET SOME SLEEP, SWEETIE–
–WE'LL TALK IN THE MORNING.

"WE'LL TALK IN THE MORNING"?
GO ON.

MY LIFE IS OVER!
THE END

UNH!
TOO HIGH!
I... CAN'T—
—GO BACK!
ALMOST GOT IT...
FLOOP
WHOOPS!
UGH!
!
Hey!
RUN
GO TO PAGE 37
GO TO DAD
GO TO PAGE 68

GOOD LUCK WITH YOUR TALENT SHOW!
THANKS, EVERYONE! GOOD LUCK AT THE SENIOR CENTER!

OH! MR. FISHER??
DO YOU HAVE ANY IDEA HOW LATE YOU ARE?
I'M SORRY. I—
AUDITORIUM BACKSTAGE
PRINCIPAL WALTHAM IS STRESSED OUT, OLIVIA IS SICK, YOU HAVE THE SCHEDULING NOTEBOOK—

IF ONLY WE'D HAD YOUR NOTEBOOK EARLIER, WE COULD—
OH NO.

I FORGOT THE NOTEBOOK!
GO TO PAGE 65

RESCUE DILLON

GO TO PAGE 151

RESCUE ANIMALS

GO TO PAGE 107

WAIT...
...I HAVE TO GET READY!
TAKE YOUR TIME— I'M OUTTA HERE!

WAIT!
JEROME!

WHAT DO I DO? WHAT DO I DO?!

I COULD TEXT FOR HELP...
TWIST
PULL

...IF MOM WOULD LET ME GET A PHONE!
GO TO PAGE 27

MRS. BELL WILL KNOW WHAT TO DO!
SHE'S PROBABLY MY KINDEST NEIGHBOR!
KNOCK
KNOCK
KNOCK
PLEASE BE HOME, PLEASE BE HOME...
TAP TAP
WAIT—MY SCOOTER! I CAN RIDE MY SCOOTER!
I HOPE OUR GARAGE ISN'T LOCKED!
HUFF
HUFF
GO TO PAGE 12

I MIGHT AS WELL DO MY HOMEWORK FOR THE NEXT WEEK WHILE I'M HOME!
-NIBBLE-
-NIBBLE-
YOU'RE RIGHT, VINCENT—
—IT'S TIME FOR A BREAK!
?
GO TO PAGE 29

A DANCE BREAK!
!
SWOOOP!
HA
HA
HA
HA
HA
HA
HA
!
OKAY, VINCENT—TIME TO GET BACK TO WORK.
-KISS-
GO TO PAGE 30

CAN'T WASTE... OPPORTUNITY...TO DO HOMEWORK...
DON'T GIVE UP ON ME NOW, VINCENT.
HMPH.
TRAITOR!
Z
CAN'T
FALL
ASLE
Z
Z
Z
GO TO PAGE 45

ONE OF THESE HAS TO UNLOCK THE CAFETERIA...
JING
CLINK
HRMM...
COME ON...

JUST OPEN! I'LL GRAB SOME NAPKINS AND BE GONE...

UNLOCK!

YES! FINALLY!

I'LL JUST GRAB THE NAPKINS AND—

OH, COME ON!
I CAN'T EVEN REACH THE OTHER LOCKS!
GO TO PAGE 73

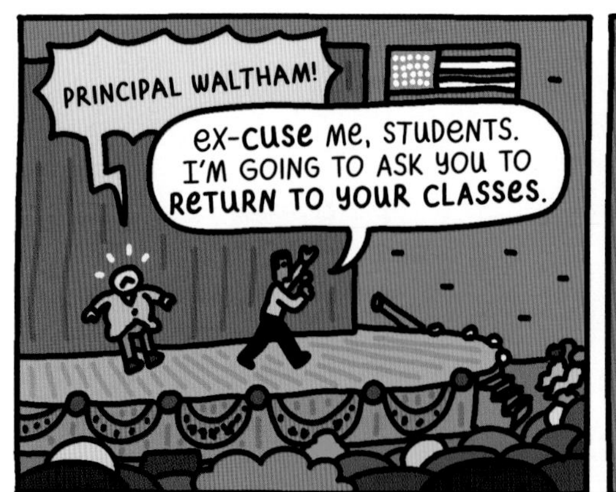
PRINCIPAL WALTHAM!
ex-CUSe Me, STUDeNTS. I'M GOING TO ASK YOU TO ReTURN TO YOUR CLASSeS.

MR. FISHeR AND I HAVe SOMe...MATTeRS TO DISCUSS.
IS THAT OKAY?

OUR SOURCeS SAY YeS!
THe eND

THERE YOU ARE!
!

DAD! YOU CAN'T JUST SNEAK UP ON PEOPLE LIKE THAT. SHEESH!

REMEMBER TO—
SNOW HUT
UGH. DAD, I KNOW...

I WILL ANNOUNCE THAT YOUR COMPANY IS SPONSORING THE TALENT SHOW AND THAT YOU'LL BE SELLING SNOW CONES—
"SNOW HUT"! SAY "BROUGHT TO YOU BY SNOW HUT"!
BYE, DAD.
SKRAW
RHOOF

PHEW!
MUNCH
MUNCH
MUNCH

SO...HUNGRY...CAN I HAVE—
WAH-CHOO!!

SORRY—WHAT?
ER...NEVER MIND...
SNRK

GO TO PAGE 34

ASK DAD TO ANNOUNCE GO TO PAGE 102
DO IT YOURSELF GO TO PAGE 82
ASK MR. FISHER GO TO PAGE 2
TELL OLIVIA TO ANNOUNCE GO TO PAGE 69

MAYBE I SHOULD HAVE WORN DIFFERENT SHOES? DO YOU THINK HE LIKES ME? IS MY HAIR OKAY? AM I DESTINED TO BECOME AN OLD ... LADY?

UM.

I'M SORRY.

I HAVE TO...

GO TO PAGE 197

GET 'EM OFF! GO AWAY!

NO, NO, NO, NO...

HA HA! HEY! STOP—
THAT TICKLES! HA HA!

EIGHTY YEARS LATER
HA HA!
SERIOUSLY—
STOP!
HA HA!
PLEASE?!
THE END

KNOCK FOR HELP
GO TO PAGE 18

FACE THE GULLS
GO TO PAGE 66

BEEP
BEEP
BOOP

YES—ONE LARGE MUSHROOM PIZZA, PLEASE. UH-HUH... SUNBRIGHT MIDDLE SCHOOL. THANKS!
?

BACKSTAGE
EW!
?
LILY, THERE'S ANOTHER!

SQUAWK! THERE'S ANOTHER!
AWK!
SHH!
GO TO PAGE 39

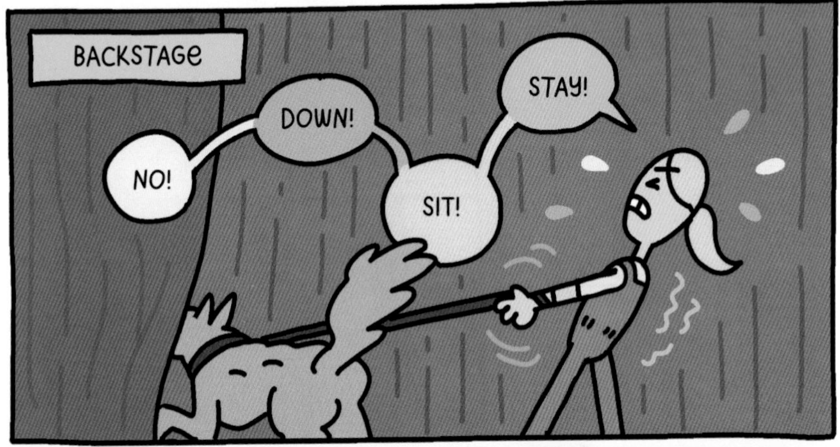

SEE WHAT MISS V WANTS
GO TO PAGE 170

STOP OLIVIA
GO TO PAGE 10

-CLIMB-
-CLIMB-
Z
JING
CLK
!
CHK
CLK
BOMP
BONG
GO TO PAGE 181

HEY!
!
SNATCH

DAD SAYS YOU'RE GROUNDED FROM VINCENT, TOO! HA HA HA!
!

I SHOULDN'T HAVE DONE ALL THAT HOMEWORK!
THE END

MEGAN!
Z Z
ZZ
Z Z

FINALLY! I THOUGHT YOU WERE DEAD.
HUH?

...JEROME?

WHAT'S WRONG WITH YOU? YOU MISSED THE BUS, AND MOM SAID I HAVE TO DRIVE YOU TO SCHOOL.
LET'S GO.

GO TO PAGE 43

ARGUE FOR MORE TIME

GO TO PAGE 26

GET READY

GO TO PAGE 57

I'M BACK, BABY!
HA
HA
HA
?
?
M...MEGAN? IS THAT YOU?
WHAT ARE YOU DOING INSIDE THE BOYS' BATH-ROOM?
DILLON PEPPER!
HE'LL NEVER LOVE A SWAMP THING!
MY LIFE IS OVER!
THE END

HIDE

GO TO PAGE 71

TELL ON JEROME

GO TO PAGE 55

GO TO PAGE 111

...A RIDE TO JAIL!

NO! PLEASE! I DIDN'T DO ANYTHING! PLEASE!
I'M INNOCENT!

KSHT
GUESS WHO JUST CAUGHT THE SUNBRIGHT BANDIT!
KSH
WANTED
UNBRIGHT
BANDIT
CONTACT POLICE
THE END

FASTER, JEROME! FASTER!
I'M TRYING! THIS CAR'S TOO OLD!
CLNK
VRRRR
CHK
CHK

CAN YOU HAND ME A HAIR TIE?
EW— WHAT THE JUNK IS THAT?

NEVER MIND.
HEY!
MY NOTEBOOK!

TIME FOR SOME TUNES.

SCREECH!!

GO TO PAGE 91

KNO
KNO
!

SOMEBODY HELP!

YOU GUYS HEAR SOMETHIN'?
?

GROSS.

ANOTHER VICTIM CLAIMED BY THE GULLS
THE END

OKAY. OLIVIA? I NEED YOU TO ANNOUNCE.
GREG—YOU'RE ON LIGHTS AND SOUND.
GOT IT!

TODD—YOU'RE ON CURTAINS.
WHAT?
-PICK-
-PICK-

AAAAAAAAAAAAAAAAAAAAAAND...

LILY!
YOU'RE IN CHARGE OF THE PERFORMERS—PEOPLE AND PETS!

CAN WE START NOW? EVERYONE'S WAITING!
MEGAN?

GO TO PAGE 33

GO TO PAGE 225

HURNGH
UHH
?
PHEW!
GREAT.
HUFF...
HUFF...
FLING
KICK
GO TO
PAGE 150

UH...UM...WELCOME—UM—STUDENTS...PARENTS...UH...UH—TO THIS YEAR'S SUNBRIGHT MIDDLE SCHOOL TALENT SHOW!
CLAP
CLAP

BROUGHT TO YOU BY SNOW HUT!

UGH. DAD...

YOU'RE DOING GREAT, LADYBUG!

HA
HA
HA
HEH HEH... O-KAY, MOM...
YEAH—KEEP GOING, LADYBUG!
HA
HA

GO TO PAGE 54

UM. **OKAY**. FIRST UP, WE HAVE...UM...**JAVIER**!
AP
CLAP

UM... **JAVI?**
CLAP

WHAT ARE YOU **DOING?**
!
SLORP!

GO AHEAD—**DO YOUR THING**. WE'RE ALL **WAITING**.
AIGHT.
15

SO, YOU KNOW HOW I SCORED **FOUR GOALS** LAST GAME?

YEAH. **THAT'S** MY TALENT.
O-**KAY**...CAN YOU **SHOW** US?
YEAH. I **DID**. IN THE **GAME**.
CLAP
CLAP
CLAP

GO TO PAGE 3

MOM!
DAD!

THERE HE IS! JEROME LEFT WITHOUT ME AND—
STOP.

DO YOU HAVE **ANY IDEA** WHAT YOUR MOTHER AND I HAVE **BEEN** THROUGH TODAY?

UM... NO?
OKAY, SWEETIE. WE **JUST** GOT HOME.

BUT **JEROME** DIDN'T EVEN **WAIT** FOR ME! I'VE BEEN WORKING ON HOMEWORK **ALL DAY** AND STRESSING ABOUT THE **TALENT SHOW**!

GO TO PAGE 22

GROUNDED?!
BUT THAT'S NOT FAIR!!

JEROME WAS SUPPOSED TO—

YOU. ARE.
GROUNDED.

AND SO...
IT'S NOT FAIR!

LOOKS LIKE IT'S JUST YOU AND ME, VINCENT.

PFFT!
WHAT DO YOU WANT?

YOU SHOULD'VE JUST COME WITH ME WHEN I WOKE YOU UP.

GO TO PAGE 41

I'M HURRYING!
I JUST HAVE TO EAT, DO MY HAIR, AND GRAB MY NOTEBOOK!
NO TIME! PICK ONE AND LET'S GO!
DO HAIR GO TO PAGE 84
EAT GO TO PAGE 5
GRAB NOTEBOOK GO TO PAGE 104

OKAY, OLIVIA—
—YOU'RE UP NEXT!
OH NO—YOU'RE STILL SICK?

...MR. TWEED?

WHAT'S...IN...THE SNOW CONES?
...THE SNOW CONES?
? ? ?

WAIT— ARE YOU ILL? I CAN'T RISK GETTING ILL!

GO TO PAGE 59

WE'LL TALK SOON!
LOOKS LIKE IT'S JUST THE TWO OF US NOW.
SQUAWK!

THERE'S SOMETHING I'VE BEEN MEANING TO TELL YOU.
?

I LOVE YOU! I LOVE YOU!
!
CLAP
CLAP
CLAP
OH NO.

OLIVIA? YOU AND YOUR PARROT ARE UP!

MR. FISHER!

LISTEN UP!
AND LISTEN GOOD.

GO TO PAGE 93

SIGH...
HOW'S IT GO?
"A JOURNEY OF A THOUSAND MILES," SOMETHING, SOMETHING??

ONE MINUTE LATER

ONE MINUTE LATER

ONE MINUTE LATER

WALKING TO SCHOOL IS GONNA TAKE FOREVER!
PLEASE TELL ME I AT LEAST HAVE SOMETHING TO READ.

WHAT? NOT EVEN A SINGLE BOOK?!

I WISH I HAD SOMETHING TO EAT...
!
GO TO PAGE 7

HUFF
HUFF
OPEN DOOR ON WALL GO TO PAGE 108
OPEN CEILING HATCH GO TO PAGE 194

STAY PUT GO TO PAGE 115
TRICK MR. FISHER GO TO PAGE 142

SUNBRIGHT HIGH SCHOOL
IT'S OPEN!
1ST
TRACK + FIELD
101

we ♥ Sunbright High!!
ENGLISH
CAN I HELP YOU?
SUNBRIGHT · SUNBRIGHT ·

HI THERE! I'M MRS. GARDENER— I'M THE ASSISTANT PRINCIPAL HERE AT SUNBRIGHT HIGH. ARE YOU A NEW STUDENT?
?

OH, HI! I'M, UH, LOOKING FOR MY OLDER BROTHER.
GO TO PAGE 64

I CAN LOOK HIM UP ON THE COMPUTER!
OFFICE

WHAT'S YOUR LAST NAME, HONEY?
HATHAWAY, MA'AM. MY BROTHER'S NAME IS—

JEROME.

YEAH! DO YOU KNOW EVERYONE'S NAMES?

NO—BUT I KNOW JEROME. HE'S DOWN THE HALL.
YOU'LL SEE HIM.
THANK YOU!

THE POOR DEAR.

GO TO PAGE 225

FAKE BEING SICK	HIDE IN BATHROOM	GIVE ASSIGNMENTS
GO TO PAGE 114	GO TO PAGE 8	GO TO PAGE 50

SQUAWK!

THAT'S RIGHT!
HA!
KNOCK ON DOOR GO TO PAGE 49
RUN TO DAD GO TO PAGE 68

GO TO PAGE 229

GO TO PAGE 117

I GUESS I DON'T REALLY HAVE A **CHOICE**...
UCK
OOG
ULG
OLIVIA?
I'M SORRY, OLIVIA—BUT I NEED YOU TO ANNOUNCE.
WHAT?!
BUT I'M NOT KIDDING!
I'M REALLY SICK!!

YOU'LL BE FINE!

WELL...SAY **SOME**THING.
?

OKAY.

ON BEHALF OF THE SUNBRIGHT MIDDLE SCHOOL STUDENT LEADERS, IT'S **MY PLEASURE** TO—

YARK!

GO TO PAGE 70

UGH...

?
OLIVIA? I'M SO SORRY—
ARE YOU OKAY?

YOU AND I NEED TO HAVE A LITTLE TALK...
!

OH NO!

THE END

GO TO PAGE 72

NO, NO, NO, NO!
HOLD IT, YOUNG LADY.
DAD! I JUST SAW— THERE'S A GHOST! OR A M-MONSTER! IT LOOKED RIGHT AT ME! PLEASE LET ME GO!

IS THAT THE GHOST-MONSTER YOU'RE RUNNING FROM?
HMM?
HA HA! DON'T YOU EVER SCARE ME LIKE THAT AGAIN!
VINCENT?!
YOU'RE GROUNDED.

GO TO PAGE 56

GO TO PAGE 177

I WILL NOW EAT THIS MUSHROOM PIZZA!

?
?
?
?
?

TODD? THIS IS YOUR TALENT?
EATING A SLICE OF PIZZA?!

CRNCH
GOLMP
THAT'S NOT ALL...

I STILL HAVE SEVEN SLICES LEFT!

UGH!
GO TO PAGE 75

GET TODD A DRINK AND NAPKINS
GO TO PAGE 141

KICK TODD OFF THE STAGE
GO TO PAGE 146

I–I DIDN'T DO ANYTHING!! I'M INNOCENT!

I GOT LOCKED IN! WELL, KIND OF...THERE WAS THIS LADDER THAT WENT ON AND ON...

I'M GONNA NEED YOU TO CALL YOUR MOM. LET'S SEE WHAT SHE HAS TO SAY.

CALL MY MOM?! PSH— I WOULD...
IF SHE'D LET ME GET MY OWN CELL!

OKAY, LOOK...

...LET ME GIVE YOU A RIDE...
GO TO PAGE 47

WH—
AAAAAAAAAAAH
WHAM!
OHHHHH...
?
HUMMMMMMM
WHAT IS THAT?
CRAWL
CRAWL
CRAWL
HUMMM
GO TO PAGE 131

YAY!
CLAP
CLAP
-WIPE-
CLAP
CLAP
GREG!
WAKE UP!
CLAP
CLAP

ENOUGH ALREADY! HE'S NOT THAT GOOD...
CLAP
CLAP
CLAP
OHHHHH...

UGH...MEGAN?
GREG. I AM SO SORRY. I CAN EXPLAIN—
WHAT'S THAT SMELL?

OKAY—TALENT SHOW OVER. EVERYONE BACK TO CLASS.
UGH.

EXCEPT FOR THE STUDENT LEADERS. I WANT YOU ALL IN MY OFFICE IN FIVE MINUTES!
GO TO PAGE 62

ANYWAY. IT'S GONNA TAKE ME ALL DAY TO WASH THE TRAYS, SO YOU'D BETTER JUST START WALKING.

START WALKING TO SCHOOL

GO TO PAGE 192

OFFER TO HELP JEROME

GO TO PAGE 228

GO TO PAGE 208

CURL
Z
Z
Z
Z
GO TO PAGE 101

ALL RIGHT—
I'LL DO IT.
I'LL NEED A HEADSET.
...NO ONE HAS A HEADSET?! HOW ARE WE SUPPOSED TO—
UM...
UH...

GRR!
OKAY...
LILY, WHO'S UP FIRST?

FIRST UP IS...JAVI!
AND WHAT'S HIS TALENT?

UM...

UH...

?
?
?

GO TO PAGE 53

GUESS I DON'T HAVE MONEY, ANYWAY...
SNIFF

OH, RALF...I'M IN NO HURRY. CAN'T YOU HELP THE POOR GIRL?
YOU KNOW I HAVE TO STICK TO THE BUS ROUTE.

AWW...JUST LOOK AT HER...
NONE OF US ARE IN A HURRY—JUST GIVE HER A RIDE!

BUT I—
OH, THE POOR DEAR!
SUCH A LONG WALK!
HAVE A HEART!
AW...
COME ON, RALFIE...
DO IT FOR ME.
TURN TO PAGE 187

AND SO...
AT LEAST MY HAIR WILL BE READY—

—EVEN IF I'M NOT!

HONK!!!

TIME'S UP!
HRMPH.
LET'S GO!
HONK
HONK

WHERE ARE MY HAIR TIES?

NICE HAIR! HA HA HA!
JUST DRIVE.
GO TO PAGE 48

WILL I BE A MILLIONAIRE?
SHAKE
SHAKE
SHAKE
SHAKE
SHAKE
CERTAINLY
I'M GONNA BE RICH!
GIVE ME THAT!
ALL RIGHT... SHOULD I QUIT?
?
YES
GRAAWGH!
CRAKK
HA
STOMP
STOMP
HA
HA
HA

GO TO PAGE 32

ERM...EXCUSE ME,
ONE MOMENT...

HERE—TAKE THIS!
YOU'RE LEAVING?!
SO WHAT AM I
SUPPOSED TO DO?
I DON'T KNOW, TODD—
MAKE SOMETHING UP!

OH BOY...

UH...UM...UH...
CAN I USE
SOMEONE'S
PHONE?

THANKS, MR. FISHER!
!

GO TO PAGE 38

SIGH...
I NEVER WOULD'VE CAUGHT THE BUS ANYWAY...
UM...
HEH HEH
ARE YOU JUST GONNA KEEP STARING AT ME?
HUH?
HEY!
GRRRR
ROWF
GO ON! GO!
GRUH
BRUFF
GO TO PAGE 88

BROOF
GRUFF
GROWR

OH NO—TRAPPED!

HUP!

OOF!

SHAME ON YOU! NAUGHTY DOGS!!

NO WAY—
SUNBRIGHT HIGH
—JEROME'S SCHOOL!
FIND JEROME AND ASK FOR A RIDE
GO TO PAGE 113
KEEP WALKING TO SCHOOL
GO TO PAGE 216

MOM!

I'M SORRY ABOUT THE TALENT SHOW.
THE IMPORTANT THING IS THAT YOU'RE SAFE.

I SHOULD WARN YOU, THOUGH...

...YOUR FATHER IS PRETTY UPSET.
GREAT...
THE END

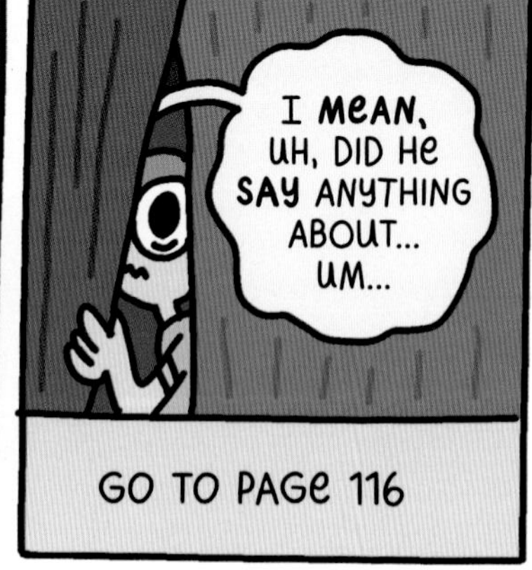

GO TO PAGE 116

SAFELY ARRIVED AT SCHOOL
THANKS FOR THE RIDE—
!
MR. FISHER?

WHERE HAVE YOU BEEN?!
EVERYONE'S BEEN LOOKING FOR YOU!
PRINCIPAL WALTHAM NEARLY HAD A HEART ATTACK!

OLIVIA HAS BEEN WORRIED SICK, THE STUDENT LEADERS ARE IN A FRENZY, THE CROWD IS RESTLESS FROM WAITING...
I-I'M SORRY? I DON'T HAVE A PHONE, SO—

AH—HERE WE ARE!
BACKSTAGE
I HOPE YOU'RE READY.

GO TO PAGE 92

MEGAN! YOU'RE HERE!
WE'RE SAVED!
?

WE COULDN'T GET HOLD OF YOU!
YOU HAVE THE NOTEBOOK WITH ALL THE INFO!

OKAY, OKAY—
SORRY I'M LATE!

NOT TO WORRY—EVERYTHING IS HERE IN MY NOTEBOOK...

IT'S NOT HERE!
WHERE DID IT GO?

GO TO PAGE 65

THIS TALENT SHOW HAS BEEN THE SINGLE GREATEST DISASTER IN SUNBRIGHT MIDDLE SCHOOL HISTORY!

I LOVE YOU.
-SKRAWK!-
I JUST CAN'T UNDERSTAND WHY—

I LOVE YOU! I LOVE YOU!
ARE YOU EVEN LISTENING TO ME?!
HEE HEE
HEE

I LOVE YOU! I LOVE YOU!
WE LOVE YOU, TOO, MR. FISHER!!
HA
HA
HA
HA
HA
HA

#$%&@
HA
HA
HA
HA

SOON
LAST ONE— HERE YA GO!
THANKS, DAD!

HERE'S TO THE BEST TALENT SHOW EVER!
CHEERS!
THE END

GO TO PAGE 181

HEY—WHO'S HAVING A GOOD TIME?
?

...

AAAAND NOW I GUESS I'M GOING TO DO A TALENT OF SOME SORT...
PLAY THE PIANO!

O-KAY...
...I WISH I'D KEPT TAKING THOSE LESSONS FROM GRANDMA.

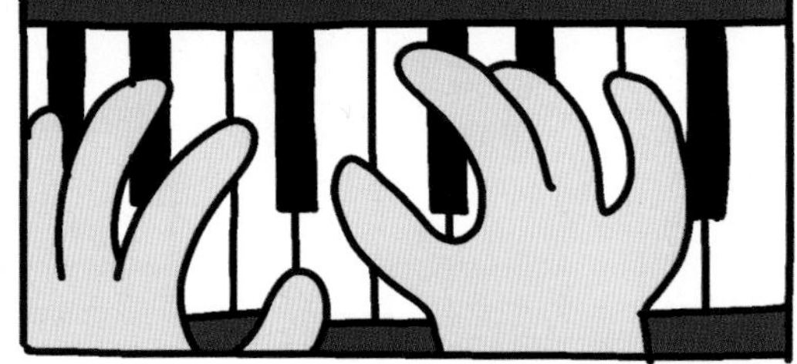

HEH HEH! I ONLY KNOW HOW TO PLAY HAPPY BIRTHDAY.

TODAY IS MY BIRTHDAY!
MINE, TOO!
AND MINE!

UM...OKAY, THEN! THIS ONE GOES OUT TO ALL THREE OF YOU...

GO TO PAGE 96

PFFT...
EASY!
I WALK UP THE STAIRS AND JUMP OUT FROM THE NEXT FLOOR.

GO TO PAGE 4

VIOLET—NO!!

I HAVE TO!
KISS
IT'S THE ONLY WAY!
KISS
KISS

GROSS.

I MISS YOU ALREADY.

AH—WELCOME BACK, VIOLET. HOW GENEROUS OF YOU TO RETURN—

JEROME HATHAWAY, GET IN HERE RIGHT THIS INSTANT!

SAVE YOURSELF, JEROME!
GO!

GO TO PAGE 16

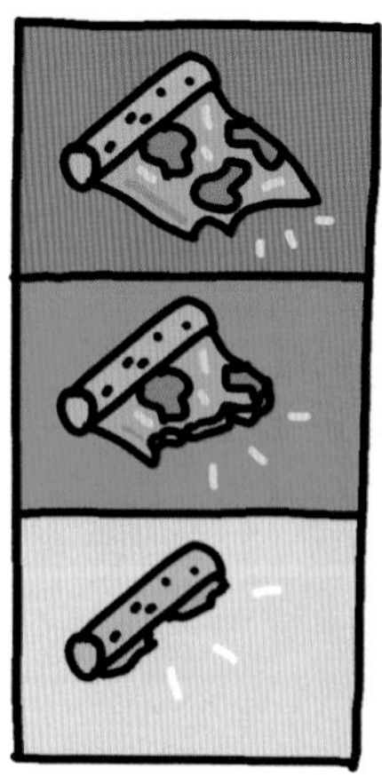

TELL OLIVIA AND HER PARROT THEY ARE NEXT

GO TO PAGE 58

END THE TALENT SHOW

GO TO PAGE 121

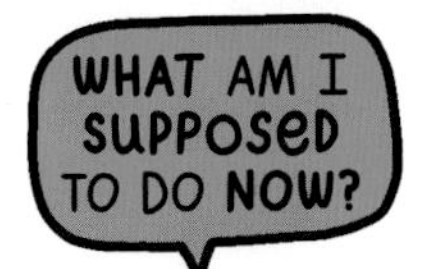

FIND ANOTHER LURE

GO TO PAGE 167

TRY TO CATCH THE PARROT

GO TO PAGE 19

HERE—TRY THIS APP I DOWNLOADED TO MR. FISHER'S PHONE!
OKAY?

ASK ME A YES OR NO QUESTION
8

GIMME THAT!

I'VE BEEN WORKING EXTRA HARD LATELY.
SHOULD I ASK FOR A RAISE?
SHAKE
SHAKE
SHAKE

MY SOURCES SAY NO

8

LET'S TRY AGAIN.
SHOULD...I...ASK... FOR...A...RAISE?!
DEFINITELY NOT
WHAT?! THIS STUPID THING'S BROKEN!
I WANNA TRY!

GO TO PAGE 85

?
SNIFF!
CLIMB OUT
GO TO PAGE 11
GO TO SLEEP
GO TO PAGE 81

ASK MR. FISHER TO ANNOUNCE

GO TO PAGE 2

ANNOUNCE YOURSELF

GO TO PAGE 82

TELL OLIVIA TO ANNOUNCE

GO TO PAGE 69

LET ME OUT!
MEGAN!

SHE—SHE WAS JUST HERE!
HUFF HUFF

GREG—CAN OTHER PEOPLE SEE "MEGAN"?
?

YOU THINK I'M MAKING HER UP? TELL HER, MR. FISHER! TELL HER THAT MEGAN IS REAL! PLEASE!
OF COURSE SHE'S REAL—BUT SHE ISN'T HERE!

GREG—THERE'S NO ONE ELSE HERE. IT'S JUST THE THREE OF US. NO MEGAN HERE.

IT'S OKAY, GREG. I USED TO HAVE A SPECIAL FRIEND, TOO.
HUH? WHAT ARE YOU TALKING ABOUT??

MAYBE WE SHOULD GIVE HIM SOME TIME ALONE...
HMM. YES.
WHERE'D YOU GO? WHERE ARE YOU?

SHE'S REAL!
SHE'S REALLY REAL!

THE END

NOW—
—WHERE DID I PUT IT?

IT'S GOTTA BE HERE...

HONK
I'M LEAVING RIGHT NOW!

ONE SECOND! I CAN'T FIND MY NOTEBOOK!
TOO BAD—I'M LEAVING.

UGH.
FINE—I'M COMING!

YOU'RE LUCKY. I ALMOST LEFT WITHOUT YOU.
GO TO PAGE 48

PUT THAT DOWN!
DON'T TOUCH THAT!
DON'T MAKE ME HOLD YOU BACK A GRADE!

!

BR-R-R-R-R!
WHAT IS THAT?
GLOOCK

GO TO PAGE 77

UM...

STOP IN THE NAME OF THE LAW!
OUCH!
OW!

HUP!

HUFF
HUFF
HUFF

OOF!

MEGAN!

MOM?

GO TO PAGE 89

OH, NO YOU DON'T—

LEAP!
GRAB!

I COMMAND YOU TO SIT—

HEY!

GROSS!
EW!
ECH!

WAIT—WHERE'S THAT PARROT?

!

GO TO PAGE 173

GO TO PAGE 109

GO TO PAGE 186

GO TO PAGE 123

HA HA
HA
HA

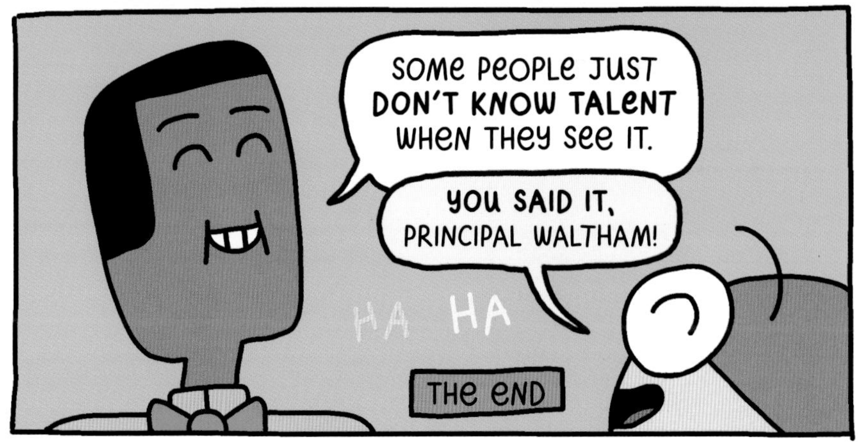
SOME PEOPLE JUST DON'T KNOW TALENT WHEN THEY SEE IT.
YOU SAID IT, PRINCIPAL WALTHAM!
HA HA
THE END

HRNGH!
HUFF!
OPEN VENT
GO TO PAGE 67
KEEP CRAWLING
GO TO PAGE 209

I ENDED UP AT JEROME'S SCHOOL, SO I MIGHT AS WELL TRY TO GET A RIDE—AGAIN!
LOCKED?
LLO?
KNOCK
CA NYONE H RME?
KNOCK
KNOCK
GO TO PAGE 63

TURN TO PAGE 36

AND YOU...
GULP!

...THE BRAINS BEHIND IT ALL!
HEH HEH HEH

I'VE BEEN WAITING FOR THIS MOMENT—
UHHH— EXCUSE ME?

SORRY TO INTERRUPT, BUT I NEED MEGAN. NOW.

DAD!
HUG
HUG
HUG

OKAY—QUICKLY! THERE ARE PAYING CUSTOMERS WAITING AT THE SNOW CONE TRUCK!

BYE!
THE END

DOES HE EVER... YOU KNOW—TALK? ABOUT ME? I NEED TO KNOW.

TALK ABOUT YOU? LIKE, IN CLASS?

OH—HI, MEREDITH! WHERE WOULD YOU LIKE TO GO TONIGHT? THE BEACH? PARIS?
HEE HEE HEE
UM.

HEE HEE HEE

MEGAN!

DO YOU THINK THIS NECKLACE IS TOO MUCH?
TOO GAUDY, MAYBE?
NOT FLASHY ENOUGH?
UMM...
GO TO PAGE 35

GO TO PAGE 118

MEGAN! PSST!

DAD?
THE TALENT SHOW—WAS IT REALLY THAT BAD?

OH NO.

DRIVE, DAD! DRIVE!

WHAT HAPPENED, ANYWAY?
LET'S TALK ABOUT IT ON THE WAY HOME.

I JUST DON'T UNDERSTAND WHY THEY'RE SO UPSET...
HERE—I'LL MAKE YOU A SNOW CONE.
THE END

UM...I CAN PLAY THE **VIOLIN**?

I CAN **SING**. KIND OF.

ABSOLUTELY **NOT**! UNDER **NO** CIRCUMSTANCES—
YES—OF COURSE! I LOVE IT!!

THIS IS HAPPENING!
HA

OKAY.
GREG.
LILY.
TODD.

I'M GONNA NEED EXTRA HELP—AND I MEAN **NOW**!
GOT IT!

LET'S **DO** IT!

PARENTS, STUDENTS, TEACHERS, AND VISITORS—**WELCOME** TO THE SUNBRIGHT MIDDLE SCHOOL TALENT SHOW—
—**PART TWO!**
CLAP
CLAP
CLAP
CLAP
GO TO PAGE 120

THANK YOU.
THANK YOU.

THE O-PEN SKY
WHOA
ellie
CAN
SING!

NINE HUNDRED AND NINETY-NINE...
ONE
THOUSAND!

CLAP
CLAP
CLAP
CLAP
CLAP

15

GO TO PAGE 6

GO TO PAGE 122

AND SO...
GET READY TO MAKE SOME MONEY, MEGAN!
I MIGHT FINALLY BE ABLE TO BUY THAT MOTORCYCLE!
UMMM... YOU KNOW MOM SAID YOU'RE NOT ALLOWED TO GET A MOTORCYCLE!
SHH—YOUR MOTHER DOESN'T NEED TO KNOW.

UPLOADED!
NOW HOW DO I TAG SOMEONE?

PLEASE TELL ME THAT'S NOT A VIDEO OF ME ONSTAGE...

HA
HA
HA
HA

STOP IT!
STOP IT RIGHT NOW!

HA HA HA! THESE VIDEOS OF MR. FISHER ARE DOPE!
HA
HA
HA
HA
HA
MR. FISHER?

BACKSTAGE
THE END

OKAY—WHAT'S YOUR NAME AND TALENT?
HOLD IT! EVERYONE STOP!
?
?
PIZZA'S HERE!
CAN I HAVE TWELVE BUCKS?
MOM?
GET BACK HERE! HE'S YOUR SON, TOO!
HERE!
I'LL PAY FOR THE PIZZA!
YOU CAN THANK ME BY PICKING UP A SNOW CONE FROM MY SNOW HUT!
GO TO PAGE 74

SERIOUSLY?!
BATHROOM CLOSED FOR CLEANING

EW! NOT SURE I NEED A QUARTER THAT BADLY...

BOYS
WET QUARTER. EW.

I NEED TO FIND ANOTHER WAY.
CAFETERIA
HMM...

I WONDER...

GO TO PAGE 31

GO TO PAGE 126

TURN TO PAGE 99

GO TO PAGE 128

WE'RE BOTH MAD. NOW CAN YOU DRIVE ME TO SCHOOL? THERE'S STILL A CHANCE I CAN MAKE IT TO THE TALENT SHOW.
PFFT!
YOU ALREADY LOST YOUR CHANCE.

THEN I'LL TELL MOM.
FINE.
TELL HER WHAT—THAT YOU DITCHED SCHOOL?

YOU DITCHED ME AND THEN YOU DITCHED CLASS TO MAKE OUT WITH A VAMPIRE!

VIOLET IS NOT A VAMPIRE!
SHE'S A SMOKIN' HOT BABE—
—AND A GOOD LISTENER AND A GENTLE SOUL!!
YOU WOULDN'T UNDERSTAND.

GO TO PAGE 79

PHEW!

TRAYS ARE DONE!
LET'S GO!

HURRY UP!!
HUFF
HUFF
HUFF
HUFF

SHOOT!
WHAT IS IT? WHAT'S WRONG?

I LEFT MY CAR KEYS BACK IN CLASS. IF I GO IN AND GET THEM, THEN MR. BARNES WILL MAKE ME STAY!
I'VE GOT THIS, BUNNY. I'LL GET THE KEYS.
BUNNY? EW!

GO TO PAGE 97

PHEW!
WHOA...
HOW LONG WAS I DOWN THERE?
GO TO PAGE 149

BRRRR!
I...
MUST BE...
IN THE...
AIR VENTS...
GO TO PAGE 112

I'M SORRY. I...I
CAN'T DO IT. I'M FULL.

WHAT?
NO.
NO!
WHERE'S MEGAN? THIS IS A WASTE OF BATTERY...

FINISH THIS PIZZA!

EAT THIS PIECE, OR I'LL SEND YOU BACK TO THIRD GRADE!
!
GO TO PAGE 98

GO TO PAGE 134

HA
HA
HA

HA!
YOU ALL LOST!
HA HA HA

YOU WERE WAY OFF!
ZEPHYR
TLSDK
QUGWI

TALENT SHOW OVER! BACK TO CLASS!
ZEPHYR
THE END

JEROME!
CALM DOWN. JEEZ.
WHAT'RE YOU DOING HERE?!
DO YOU HAVE ANY IDEA WHAT I'VE BEEN THROUGH?!

MOM SAID I HAVE TO GIVE YOU A RIDE, BUT WE HAVE TO GO OUT BACK 'CAUSE SOME DUMB BIRD IS TRAPPED IN THE FRONT.
CLINK!

REALLY?
IS IT A PARROT?
?

WE HAVE TO STOP AT OLIVIA'S ON THE WAY HOME!
UGH.
THE END

GRR
CHOMP!
TAIL
!
?
GO TO PAGE 21

GO TO PAGE 138

GO TO PAGE 162

IT'S A ROWDY LIFE FOR ME
DON'T WANNA BE TRIPPIN'

LOOKIN' ROUND FOR FOOD TO FEED MY CREW!
STAY 'WAY FROM THA ROWDIES OR WE'LL EAT YOU!

I HAVE TO WASH MY BRAIN!

ROWDY GIRLS!!
THIS IS YOUR STOP, YOUNG LADY!
GO TO PAGE 24

CONTINUE DOWNSTAIRS
GO TO PAGE 214

TURN AROUND AND LEAVE
GO TO PAGE 185

GO TO PAGE 212

YOU'RE GOING TO **LOVE** THE PUNISHMENT I **PICKED FOR YOU**...
YAAAAAAWN!
HUH?

HUH? WHAT ARE YOU **DOING?**
YAWN!
YAWN!
YAAAAAWN!

STOP IT!
STOP IT RIGHT NOW!

I **TOLD** YOU—Y-Y-
YAAAAAAAAWN!
HEE HEE HEE
???
YAWN!
YAWN!
YAWN!
YAWN!
GO TO PAGE 143

IT'S NOT FUNNY! STOP—I'M IN CHARGE!
HA
HA
HA
HA

I'M—YAWN—GOING TO—YAWN—HOLD YOU—YAWN—BACK...
!

...ZZZ...

HA HA! MEETING'S OVER!
?
AND THE PARTY BEGINS!
Z
-POKE
-POKE

GREAT WORK TODAY, TEAM!
PRINCIPAL WALTHAM!
Z...
HA
HA
YAY!
THE END

GO TO MEGAN'S ROOM
GO TO PAGE 172
GO TO JEROME'S ROOM
GO TO PAGE 94

GO TO PAGE 80

GO TO PAGE 147

HMM...
HOW 'BOUT THIS?
TODD!
TODD!

JUST A FEW BITES LEFT!
TODD!
TODD!
TODD!
TODD!

MEGAN! PSST—HEY!
OH NO— MISS V?
SEE WHAT MISS V WANTS
GO TO PAGE 90
IGNORE MISS V
GO TO PAGE 197

GO TO PAGE 133

TALK WITH OFFICER
GO TO PAGE 76

RUN
GO TO PAGE 106

WHERE'S THE LIGHT?

GREAT.
WHERE AM I?

SIGH...

AND **NOW** I'M GOING UP **ANOTHER** CREEPY OLD LADDER...**GREAT!**
GO TO PAGE 194

GO TO PAGE 152

GO TO PAGE 202

GO TO PAGE 154

THREE HOURS LATER...
"...TO THE MOANING AND THE GROANING OF THE BELLS."
THANK YOU.

Z
Z
Z
Z

HEY—WAKE UP! ALL OF YOU!
IS THIS ANY WAY TO TREAT YOUR SUPERIOR?!
Z
Z
Z
Z

THAT'S IT! NONE OF YOU ARE LEAVING UNTIL YOU CAN APPRECIATE POETRY! GOT IT?
?
?

I DON'T CARE IF YOU HAVE JOBS OR NEED TO SLEEP OR GO TO THE BATHROOM—YOU'RE ALL STAYING HERE UNTIL I SAY YOU CAN GO!
THE END

UM...DOES **ANYBODY** HAVE A TALENT TO SHARE?

OH...
...NO.
GO TO PAGE 46

UM...
IT'S MINE!
YEAH!
UP HERE!

THANKS! HEY—DO YOU HAPPEN TO HAVE MORE? LIKE, A BUNCH?
ACTUALLY, WE JUST HAD THIS HUGE ORDER CANCEL ON US. GIMME ONE MINUTE!

HEY—
—WHO'S READY FOR SOME YO-YO?

WHOOPS!
SPZZ
OKAY, NOW I...
SWOP
NOPE.
WHOOP!
HOLD ON...
FLOOP
HA HA HA HA HA

OH, GOOD— JUST IN TIME...
PIZZA'S HERE!
?

GO TO PAGE 14

GIRL IN THE SKIRT
GO TO PAGE 123

BOY IN SPARKLES
GO TO PAGE 110

I HAVE ANOTHER IDEA! CHARLOTTE ALWAYS SAYS I GIVE GREAT ADVICE...
SO—WHO WANTS SOME ADVICE?

WELL, THERE'S THIS GIRL I LIKE—BUT I DON'T KNOW IF SHE LIKES ME, AND I DON'T KNOW WHAT TO DO.

SO TELL HER!! I MEAN, COME ON—LIFE'S TOO SHORT TO PLAY GAMES WITH THE HEART. GOT IT?

YOU'RE RIGHT.

IZZY—IT'S YOU! I'VE LIKED YOU EVER SINCE YOU GAVE ME YOUR MASHED POTATOES BACK IN THE FIRST GRADE.
?
YOINK
GO TO PAGE 159

YOU LIKE ME?? WOW! OKAY, UM...WELL...

I LIKE YOU, TOO!

ANYONE ELSE LOOKING FOR ADVICE?
TINA?

YES—THANK YOU. I AM CONCERNED FOR MY FUTURE. IS A ROTH IRA WORTH THE INVESTMENT, OR SHOULD I BE LOOKING INTO A 401(K)?

HOLD UP—YOU NEED TO THINK ABOUT THE IMPORTANT THINGS, OKAY? LIKE, HOW ARE YOU GOING TO GET THROUGH PUBERTY?
WHO ELSE?
GO TO PAGE 190

FIVE MINUTES LATER, AT SUNBRIGHT MIDDLE SCHOOL...
GOOD LUCK, LADYBUG! I'M GONNA GET STARTED ON THE SNOW CONES.
THANKS, DAD!

THERE YOU ARE!

WE'VE BEEN WAITING FOR YOU ALL MORNING!
I'M SORRY, MR. FISHER. I—

IT WOULD BE REALLY HELPFUL IF YOU HAD A CELL PHONE!
TELL ME ABOUT IT!
GO TO PAGE 92

A FLASHLIGHT!

IT STILL WORKS!
CLICK!
HMM...
WHAT'S THIS?

OOH—THE ADVENTURE CONTINUES!
EXPLORE TUNNEL
GO TO PAGE 178
CLIMB LADDER
GO TO PAGE 205

ADMIT THE SHOW NOTES ARE LOST
GO TO PAGE 213

END THE TALENT SHOW
GO TO PAGE 171

THAT SHOULD DO IT.
CAN YOU ALL SEE OKAY?
HERE IS MY LITTLE LADYBUG.
SHE HATED WEARING CLOTHES!
SHE'S NAKED!
HA HA HA HA HA

MOM—WHAT ARE YOU DOING?!
NOW, THIS IS WHEN SHE CAUGHT THAT TERRIBLE RASH—REMEMBER THAT? I THOUGHT IT'D NEVER LEAVE.

LATER
...AND THAT'S MY LADYBUG!
MEGAN?
YAY!
WOW!
HA HA HA!

HA HA
YOUR MOM IS SO FUNNY!
SEE YOU IN CLASS, LADYBUG!
OUTSIDE THE AUDITORIUM
MY LIFE IS OVER.
THE END

GO TO PAGE 103

GO TO PAGE 166

OLIVIA!
IT'S YOU!

OLIVIA? HEY, IT'S ME—MEGAN...
ARE YOU OKAY?

SLAM!!
HEY!

OOMF!
?
EXPLORE TUNNEL GO TO PAGE 13
REACH IN HOLE GO TO PAGE 161

UGH—
—THERE'S NO FOOD AROUND!

OKAY, MEGAN—DON'T MESS THIS UP. LOOK WITHIN AND SING YOUR HEART SONG.
BELIEVE AND THE PARROT WILL WALK RIGHT INTO THE—

!

THE PARROT IS GONE!
I LOST THE POOR BIRD!
I'M THE WORST!

...MEGAN?
HUH?
GO TO PAGE 168

OLIVIA!
YOU AREN'T SICK ANYMORE!
YEAH!
I THINK IT WAS THE 24-MINUTE FLU.

OLIVIA—I'M SO SORRY! I LOST YOUR PARROT! I'M THE WORST!

YOU MEAN THIS PARROT?

OH, OLIVIA! YOU FOUND THE BIRD!
HIDE-AND-SEEK IS HIS FAVORITE GAME!

YOU CAN RIDE HOME WITH ME. OH—WANT SOME NUTS? IT'S ALL HE EATS. HA HA!
UM—IT'S NOT ALL HE EATS.
THE END

GO TO PAGE 201

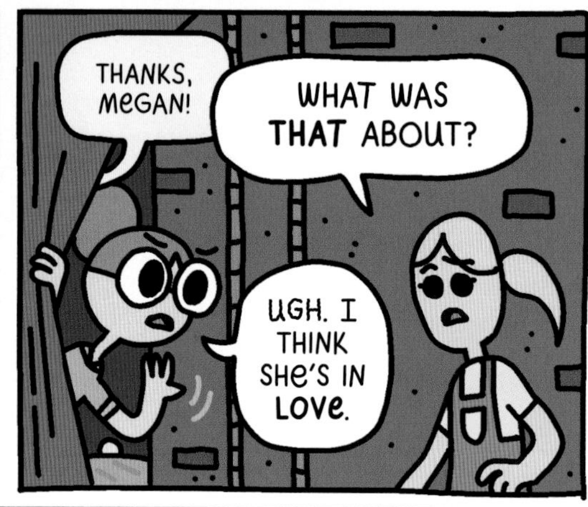

STOP OLIVIA

GO TO PAGE 203

PASS MISS V'S NOTE TO MR. TWEED

GO TO PAGE 210

GO TO PAGE 119

GO TO PAGE 40

TURN TO PAGE 174

STOP THE CROWD
GO TO PAGE 227

FOLLOW THE PARROT
GO TO PAGE 125

GO TO PAGE 176

ALL RIGHT, ALL RIGHT. ENOUGH OF THAT— WHATEVER IT'S SUPPOSED TO BE...
SHOW'S OVER.
WHAT?!
NO!
UGH!
WHY?

AND YOU ALL GET EXTRA HOMEWORK!
HA!
LET'S SEE YOU CLAP FOR THAT!

WORTH IT!!
HA HA HA HA HA HA HA HA HA HA HA HA HA HA HA HA
THE END

BEEP!
.80/
1.00
COME ON...

STILL NOTHING?

ALL RIGHT, NAPKINS—
I'M COMING FOR YOU!

HRNGH!
HRMF!

JUST
A LITTLE
CLOSER...
GO TO PAGE 204

COOOOL!
I WONDER WHAT'S IN—

—SPIDER!!

OOPS.

THIS IS SO GROSS...
WHAT AM I STEPPING IN?
CROAK
CHIP
CHIP
CHIP

ew.
ew.
ew.
SQUEAK!

GO TO PAGE 13

GO TO PAGE 180

UGH...
?
...MEGAN?

WHAT'S HAPPENED? WHAT'S GOING ON—
SHHHH— NOTHING. QUIET.

WE HAVE YOU SURROUNDED. COME OUT WITH YOUR HANDS UP.

WHAT IS HAPPENING RIGHT NOW?! DID WE DO SOMETHING WRONG?!

WE SHOULD PROBABLY DO WHAT THEY SAY.

I NEED YOU BOTH TO CLIMB DOWN. YOU'RE GOING TO JAIL.
THE END

-SNIFF-
-SNIFF-
GO TO PAGE 101

SEND OUT TALENT

GO TO PAGE 157

HELP TODD

GO TO PAGE 95

GO TO PAGE 184

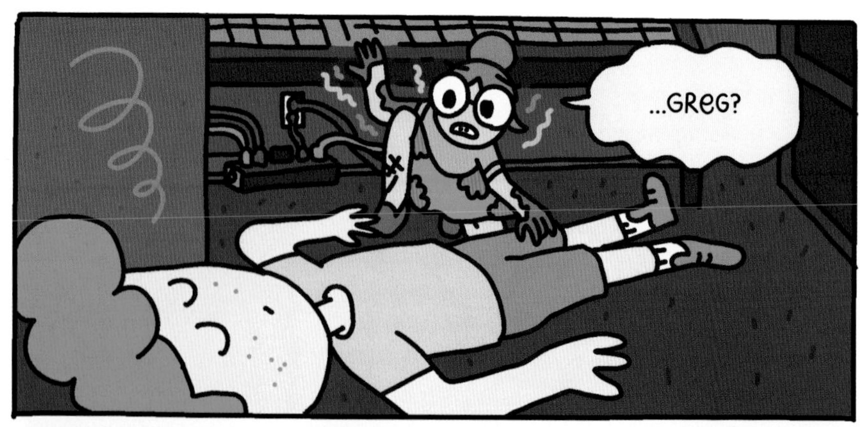

WATCH JEROME
GO TO PAGE 220

WAKE GREG
GO TO PAGE 78

CREEAK
MR. TWEED?

HEY, MR. TWEED! HAVE YOU SEEN OLIVIA?
HUH? I'M TRYING TO CALL MISS V... WHY WON'T SHE ANSWER?!

GIGGLE! GIGGLE!

HERE, MR. TWEED. THIS MIGHT HELP—
MEGAN!
COME QUICK!

COME ON! WE HAVE TO HURRY!
HELLO? HELLO?
GO TO PAGE 218

GO TO PAGE 183

GO TO PAGE 139

FIFTY YEARS LATER...
HELLO? OLIVIA?
SQUIK

GREG?
JEROME?
MR. FISHER?

...ANYONE?

THE END

WOW!
CLAP
CLAP
CLAP

NO WAY!
CHECK IT OUT!
CLAP

CLAP
CLAP
CLAP
CLAP

THANK YOU! YEAH! HEY—LET'S CHANGE THE SCHOOL NAME TO ERASTUS R. FISHER MIDDLE SCHOOL!
WHO'S WITH ME? HUH?

NOBODY??? SERIOUSLY?!

ALL RIGHT, THEN—SHOW'S OVER! BACK TO CLASS!

UGH!

LAME.

STRANGE MAN, BUT WHAT TALENTED FEET!

THE END

GO TO PAGE 191

GO TO PAGE 100

FORGET IT!
I'LL JUST WALK ALONE.
THE POOR DEAR.
HERE, MEGAN— THESE ARE FOR YOU.
GIRL, YOU KNOW I LIKE YOU.
HONK!
HUH?!
GO TO PAGE 221

I'M SORRY—
?
BUT THE **SCHOOL** ISN'T EVEN **ON MY ROUTE**!

I'LL **NEVER** MAKE IT TO SCHOOL!

SOB
SNIFF
SOB

I'M **VERY SORRY**, BUT I **HAVE** TO STICK TO THE ROUTE...
IT'S MY **JOB**!

GO TO PAGE 83

CRK
CRRRRR
COME ON...
CROOO
DOONK
GO TO PAGE 130

GO TO PAGE 196

LISTEN TO MR. FISHER'S IDEA
GO TO PAGE 148

COME UP WITH A NEW IDEA
GO TO PAGE 158

GO TO PAGE 198

YOU'RE UP!
ONE MORE SLICE! ONE MORE SLICE!
GO GET 'EM!

ONE MORE SLICE!
ONE MORE SLICE!
ONE MORE SLICE!

I CAN'T DO IT...
...I'M FULL.

YOU'VE GOT THIS, TODD! JUST ONE MORE SLICE.
I'M GONNA YARK.

HMM...
ENCOURAGE TODD TO FINISH
GO TO PAGE 132
ASK FOR MORE TALENT
GO TO PAGE 155

SUNBRIGHT

OLIVIA! I'M SO SORRY—I LOST YOUR PARROT! HE FLEW OUT THE DOOR, AND—AND—AND NOW HE'S GONE!
THIS WAY, SWEETIE—WE'LL GET YOU SOME HELP.

I'M ONLY GONNA SAY THIS ONCE...

...I'M A PRETTY PONY.
?
?
?
AHA! THERE YOU ARE.
GO TO PAGE 200

I **JUST** HAD THE MOST PLEASANT CONVERSATION WITH YOUR **PARENTS**...
ARE YOU TALKING TO **ME**?

THEY SAID YOU CAN STAY TO HELP ME **CLEAN THE AUDITORIUM.**

IT'S GOING TO TAKE **ALL DAY**, YOU KNOW.

WE'LL HAVE **PLENTY** OF TIME TO **TALK**...

HAVE **I** EVER TOLD YOU ABOUT MY FAMILY'S **MEDICAL HISTORY**?

UGH!

THE END

GO TO PAGE 124

HUH?
GRAB

LET'S GO TO THE SNOW CONE TRUCK.
?

HEY! YOU CAN'T LEAVE!

I PAID FOR THIS MESS! I CAN DO WHATEVER I WANT!

WHAT A WEIRD DAY.
THE END

WHERE'D OLIVIA GO?!

SHE'S GONE! GREAT. OKAY, MEGAN...KEEP IT TOGETHER...

WHERE IS SHE?!
SHE WAS BY THE CHANGING ROOMS A MINUTE AGO.
SIT!
GOOD BOY.

YOU SURE?
I JUST SAW HER, LIKE, TWO SECONDS AGO.

OLIVIA?
OPEN THE TRAPDOOR
GO TO PAGE 140
OPEN THE BACK DOOR
GO TO PAGE 185

HA!
GOTCHA!
OKAY—PHEW! I CAN'T BELIEVE I'M REALLY DOING THIS.
EWWW!
YAY!
CHEER!
HOORAY!
HUH?! WHAT'S HAPPENING?
I'M COMING!
BACK TO THE AUDITORIUM!
HUFF
GO TO PAGE 197

KEEP CLIMBING

GO TO PAGE 61

CLIMB DOWN

GO TO PAGE 222

GO TO PAGE 207

CLAIM THE PIZZA
GO TO PAGE 156

REFUSE THE PIZZA
GO TO PAGE 175

BARK
BARK
?
BAR! BAR!
BAR!
BAR!
BAR!
!
BAR!
BAR!
BAR!
GO TO PAGE 136

S-S-SSSO C-CCOL-LD...
HUHH
HUNHH
HNGH!
HUFF HUHH
PHEW!
DOES THIS EVER END??
GO TO PAGE 52

OKAY, OKAY. JUST LET ME DELIVER THIS FIRST.
THERE HE IS!

PSSSST!
MR. TWEED!
HEY!
TAP-TAP-

OLIVIA?? WHERE'D YOU COME FROM?

WILL YOU HOLD THIS FOR ME?
UM...HMM...ARE YOU FEELING ALL RIGHT?

WHAT ARE YOU DOING?!
NOM
NOM
GO TO PAGE 211

GO TO PAGE 182

EVERYONE LIKES ROOT BEER...
...RIGHT?
25¢
25¢
25¢
.75/1.00
OH, SHOOT— I'M ALL OUT OF QUARTERS.
PAT
PAT
PAT
PAT
NOTHING IN THE RETURN?
OH, COME ON...
GO TO PAGE 169

GO TO PAGE 163

...OLIVIA?
ARE YOU DOWN HERE?
SCREEECH!
WHAT IS THIS PLACE?
STEP
STEP
STEP
GO TO PAGE 215

HMM?
WHAT'S IN THERE?
WAIT A MINUTE...
...ANOTHER TUNNEL?
SHOUT FOR HELP
GO TO PAGE 165
ENTER TUNNEL
GO TO PAGE 13
LOOK IN HOLE
GO TO PAGE 161

UGH! I BET I COULD STILL WALK TO SCHOOL FASTER THAN I COULD TALK JEROME INTO DRIVING ME!
HMM...
I THINK SCHOOL IS THIS WAY...
JEROME THINKS HE'S SO COOL.
PSH!
HEY!
!
FOLLOWING
ME!
STOP
GO TO PAGE 217

HUFF
WHAT
DO YOU
HUNHH
HUHH
HUFF
WANT
FROM
ME?
HUFF
HUHH

THERE IS NO ESCAPE.

YOU CAN'T RUN FROM
THE GULL!

HRAUGH!

HUFF
HUHH
HUNH
GO TO PAGE 9

GO TO PAGE 206

SNIFF
SNIFF
MN
NM
NM
GO TO PAGE 145

GO TO PAGE 230

GO TO PAGE 160

GO TO PAGE 188

GO TO PAGE 224

GO TO PAGE 129

TALK TO JEROME

GO TO PAGE 127

RUSH TO BATHROOM

GO TO PAGE 51

WAIT FOR Me!

Hey!
WAIT!

POUND!
POUND!
POUND!

SCReeeCH!!

HUFF HUFF
CAN YOU...TAKe Me...
TO SUNBRIGHT...
MIDDLe SCHOOL?
GO TO
PAGe 193

STOP—PLEASE!
EVERYONE JUST WAIT—

?

SNIFF

WOOSH
!

SUNBRIGHT
WAIT!
NO!!!
GO TO PAGE 199

GUH. FINE—I'LL HELP.
DIDN'T YOU HEAR ME? IT'LL TAKE FOREVER!
SMOOCH!

ALL THREE OF US CAN HELP!
IT'S NOT HAPPENING!
AWW, IS JER-BEAR UPSET?

THEN I'M TELLING MOM!
HERE—I'LL KISS IT ALL BETTER.

UGH...
?
...FINE.
YES!!
GO TO PAGE 223

B-R-R-R-R!
SURE IS COLD IN HERE!
EW—AND SO MANY BUGS!
OF COURSE IT'S LOCKED...
CLK! CLK!
WHOOPS!
NO...
NO!!
LET ME OUT!
POUND
PLEASE!
HELP!
GO TO PAGE 164

UNLOCK DOOR

GO TO PAGE 179

SLIP OUT THE HATCH

GO TO PAGE 105

HOW TO DRAW

1. DRAW A CIRCLE.

HEAD

2. DRAW TWO SMALLER CIRCLES IN THE MIDDLE.

(SHOULD LOOK LIKE A PIG'S SNOUT)

OINK!

3. ADD EYES.

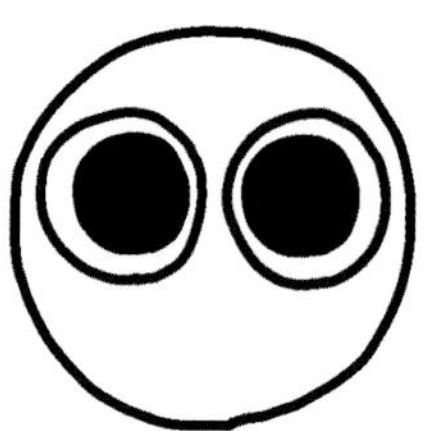

4. CONNECT MEGAN'S HAIR AND GLASSES.

STRAIGHT LINES ON THE SIDES AND IN THE MIDDLE

DON'T FORGET MEGAN'S HAIRLINE!

5. ADD BUN TO HEAD.

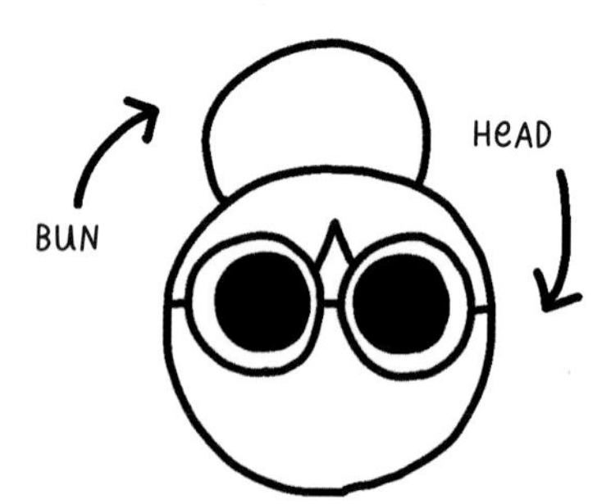

6. ADD A HAPPY SMILE AND EYEBROWS.

HOW TO DRAW

1. DRAW A TALL AND ROUNDED RECTANGLE.

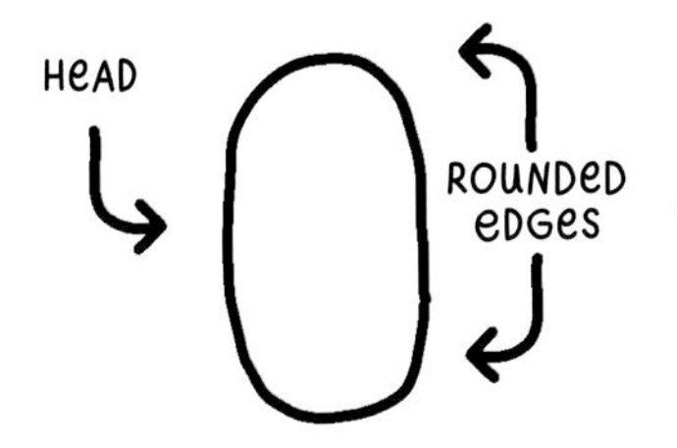

2. ADD A POOF OF HAIR.

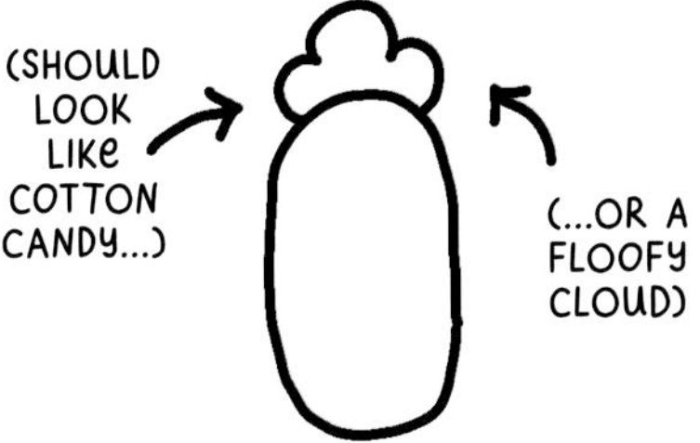

3. ADD AN ANGRY "V."

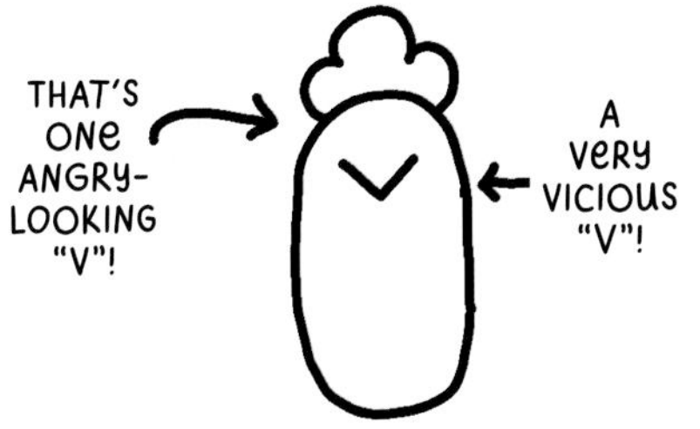

4. ADD EYES BENEATH THE ANGRY "V."

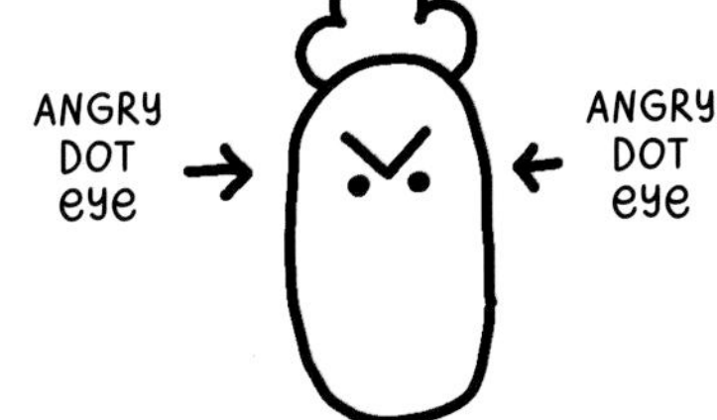

5. ADD ANGRY FROWN.

6. ADD FRECKLES ACROSS FACE.

NICE WORK!

LOOKS GREAT!

CONTINUE THE ADVENTURE IN...

WHAT HAPPENS NEXT?

YOU DECIDE THE STORY!

OVER 100 PATHS!

Science Fair Frenzy

JESS SMART SMILEY